DOCTOR ·

THE DARKSMITH LEGACY

BBC CHILDREN'S BOOKS
Published by the Penguin Group
Penguin Books Ltd, 80 Strand, London, WC2R 0RL, England
Penguin Group (USA) Inc., 375 Hudson Street, New York 10014, USA
Penguin Books (Australia) Ltd, 250 Camberwell Road, Camberwell, Victoria 3124, Australia
(A division of Pearson Australia Group Pty Ltd)
Canada, India, New Zealand, South Africa
Published by BBC Children's Books, 2009
Text and design © Children's Character Books, 2009
This edition produced for The Book People Ltd,
Hall Wood Avenue, Haydock, St Helens, WA11 9UL
Written by Jacqueline Rayner
Cover illustration by Peter McKinstry
1
ISBN: 9781405906661
Printed in Great Britain by Clays Ltd, St Ives plc

# DOCTOR · WHO

# THE DARKSMITH LEGACY

## THE PICTURES OF EMPTINESS

### BY JACQUELINE RAYNER

Book
8

The Darksmith adventure continues online. Log on to
the website, enter the special codes from your book
and enjoy games and exclusive content about
*The Darksmith Legacy.*

www.**thedarksmithlegacy**.com

# Contents

# The Story So Far...

The Doctor has taken the powerful Eternity Crystal from the terrible Darksmith Collective on the planet Karagula. The Crystal can create life, and the Doctor knows it mustn't be allowed to fall into the wrong hands. The Darksmiths need the Crystal to fulfil their contract to create a device for a mysterious client.

With the help of Gisella – the robotic 'daughter' of Varlos, the Darksmith who created the Crystal – the Doctor tries to find out who the Darksmiths are working for. The people who commissioned the Crystal are the only ones who know how to destroy it.

But after an exciting adventure on an Orbit Station above the planet Ursolonamex, the Doctor and Gisella rush back to the TARDIS to escape from the Darksmiths' military police force – the Dreadbringers. They hope data from the Orbit Station will tell them where the Darksmiths mysterious allies went...

# Captured

They were back in the TARDIS, safe from the searching Dreadbringers. The TARDIS had finished analysing the surveillance data from Orbit Station 3's systems. But all it showed was a massive energy surge as the mysterious attackers had fired their weapons.

The Doctor tapped the TARDIS screen. 'There's a trail, an energy trace from their engines. So we know where one of the ships that was involved went after the attack on Ursolonamex.'

'But that's great,' Gisella told him. 'That means we can follow them.'

The Doctor nodded. 'True. But we didn't really need this data to find out where they're headed. But I'm glad we came. If we hadn't been here, the Dravidians wouldn't have discovered anything useful either, but they might still have destroyed the Orbit Station and killed Commander Sarla and everyone else.'

'You said we didn't need the data to know where the attackers went,' Gisella said. 'Why's that? Do you know where they were going?'

'Could have guessed,' the Doctor said. 'The energy trail leads back to Karagula. The planet of the Darksmiths. So we still don't know who they are working for or how to destroy the Eternity Crystal.'

'Then we need a new plan,' Gisella told him. 'We can't just give up. However risky and dangerous it might be, we have to do something.'

The Doctor was busily setting the TARDIS controls. 'You're absolutely right,' he said. 'Nice trick with the fire extinguisher, by the way. Good thinking.'

'Thanks.'

'Right, all set.' The Doctor operated the control that opened the TARDIS doors. 'Just one more little thing for me to do, and then the TARDIS is off to Karagula.'

'Where are you going?' Gisella asked as the Doctor headed for the doors.

'Outside. Just for a minute. There's nothing to worry about. Just one last thing I need to do before we go.'

The Doctor stepped into the docking area, carefully closing the TARDIS door behind him. He took a deep breath and nodded happily. Chief Engineer Tyrall had turned up the oxygen again. Soon Orbit Station 3 would be getting back to normal.

He turned back to the TARDIS.

And strong arms grabbed him as a Dreadbringer stepped out of the shadows. Its armoured helmet was so close to the Doctor's face he could see his reflection in the polished surface.

'At last we have you, Doctor,' the Dreadbringer rasped. 'You are our prisoner, and there can be no escape this time!'

Many hours later, the Doctor was led into a round room. Tiers of benches encircled a central dais, and rows of orange lights glowed from a domed ceiling. The Doctor felt like he was standing in a hollowed-out pumpkin. The rows of skeletal Darksmiths staring at him from the benches only reinforced the Hallowe'en impression; when the Adjudicator arrived the Doctor half expected him to say 'Trick or treat?'

He didn't, of course. He was a member of the Shadow Proclamation, and as such extremely dignified. And the Doctor was very pleased to see him.

He was the reason the Time Lord had allowed himself to be captured.

It wasn't that the Doctor really minded being on the run. It happened so often that he sometimes found it a bit boring if no one was chasing him. But when he had an important job on hand – like destroying the dangerously powerful Eternity Crystal – relentless pursuers could really get in the way. How much easier if they were called off.

The Shadow Proclamation were just the beings to do that.

The Doctor had realized that if the Darksmiths had now officially involved their Dreadbringers, then everything would have to be done properly – completely above board. In an affair this big, he had hoped that meant a representative of the Shadow Proclamation would be involved, and he was relieved to discover that he'd been right. OK, so he might not get away with much under the Adjudicator's stern eye – which didn't mean that he wouldn't try – but at least his trial would be fair.

And the Doctor being the Doctor, he might just have a trick or two up his sleeve...

Once on the dais, the Doctor's two glass-fleshed warders let go of him and retired to a front bench. He rubbed his forearms and looked around for a seat. Obligingly, a white shape began to form out of the floor behind him. He sank back into it as it moulded itself to his body, while at the other end of the dais, a similar structure was preparing itself for the Adjudicator. However, while the Adjudicator's chair kept growing up and up, allowing the judge to look down on the defendant and the surrounding Darksmiths, the Doctor's not only remained low, but also shaped itself around his limbs, creating white plasticky cuffs that gripped his forearms and calves.

'Hey!' he called out in surprise, as he found himself unable to move – but thought better of protesting too much. At least the moulded chair meant that he was comfortable, which certainly hadn't been the case for most of his courtroom appearances. Really, he did seem to be put on trial an awful lot for someone who was only ever trying to help...

'The defendant will give his name and designation,' boomed the Adjudicator.

'Certainly, your shadowy honour,' said the

Doctor with a polite nod. 'I am known as the Doctor, the last of the Time Lords of Gallifrey.'

A murmur passed round the courtroom, spinning dizzily through the massed Darksmiths. Not all of them had known who – or rather, what – they were dealing with. The Doctor smiled slightly inside. Any advantage...

The pale Adjudicator, however, coolly professional, gave no start of recognition, no gasp of horror. 'Relate the charge, High Minister Drakon,' he said, addressing a tall Darksmith, the only one who had a seat on the dais.

Drakon rose to his feet. 'The charge is theft of Darksmith property, namely the so-called Eternity Crystal,' he said.

'Not guilty!' called the Doctor.

Drakon glared. 'There can be no question of your guilt. The Crystal has been in your possession for the last three-hundred vectors!'

'Hey!' The Doctor turned to the Adjudicator. 'He's prejudicing the trial! I'm innocent until proven guilty, m'lud.'

The Adjudicator raised a hand, but said nothing. He seemed to be processing information. The Doctor, who had expected just to be told to be quiet, was slightly taken aback.

Finally the Adjudicator spoke. 'Innocent until proven guilty. A legal standard found on 87 member planets and 12932 affiliated worlds. This form of trial is acceptable under Article 1768C. The court will proceed in accordance with this directive.' He paused for a moment, blinked and resumed his previous expression, then he turned to Drakon. 'The trial will begin. State your evidence.'

But the Doctor's head was churning with new ideas. 'Ooh, wait wait wait,' he called, trying but failing to raise a hand to attract the judge's attention.

The Adjudicator looked at him. 'Yes?'

'Itchy nose,' said the Doctor. 'Could the court appoint someone to scratch it?'

The Adjudicator ignored him. 'The trial will begin,' he repeated pointedly.

'Ooh, wait wait wait,' the Doctor called again.

'The accused is wasting the court's time!' shouted Drakon.

'I most certainly am not,' replied the Doctor indignantly, having gained the few seconds he needed to process his thoughts. 'If anything, I'm saving it time. Do I understand correctly' – he turned to the Adjudicator – 'that under Article

1768C, any legitimate trial form may be used in a Shadow Proclamation hearing?'

'If appropriate and approved by a majority of recognized legal systems,' agreed the Adjudicator.

'Good,' said the Doctor. 'Then I demand to be tried by a jury of my peers.' He tried to fold his arms defiantly, but was again fooled by the chair. He touched his fingertips to each other defiantly instead.

Once more, the Adjudicator seemed to be assessing this request. After a few seconds, he spoke. 'Trial by jury of peers. A legal standard found on 298 member planets and 39761 affiliated worlds. This form of trial is acceptable under Article 1768C. The court will proceed in accordance with this directive.' He blinked hard. 'A jury of the defendant's peers must be assembled before this trial can commence.'

The Doctor gave a sad smile. It was rare that the most terrible thing that had ever happened to him could be used for something positive. 'I'm afraid, Mr Adjudicator, that that's impossible. I think I did mention that I'm the *last* of the Time Lords. Unless you can come up with a dozen other thousand-year-old regenerating masters of time and space... well, I can't be tried by my peers.

I move for a mistrial, case dismissed!'

Confident of victory, the Doctor allowed himself a proper smile, especially when he saw the expression of rage on the face of Drakon.

But his smugness was short-lived.

The Adjudicator did not even have to consult his mental databanks.

'When the requested form of trial is impossible, judgement reverts to Shadow Proclamation standard,' he informed the Doctor. 'Trial will therefore commence in this manner.'

'No, wait!' The Doctor wasn't going to give up that easily. 'How about something else, then? I know, trial by combat! Me versus Drakon at tiddlywinks! Or a pie-eating contest – as long as they're something nice like apple, that is. Or cherry – how d'you feel about cherry pie, Drakon?'

The High Minister of the Darksmiths looked like he might explode. But the Adjudicator stepped in before the Doctor could continue. For once, he sounded almost sympathetic, not as coldly efficient as usual. 'The defendant has submitted his maximum two requests,' he said. 'Shadow Proclamation standard will be adopted. Doctor, your trial will now begin.'

The Doctor sighed. It had been a long shot, anyway. And to be honest, he was almost looking forward to the trial. He was hoping to find out the answers to a few questions...

# Help Arrives

**D**rakon was the first to speak. The Doctor listened intently as the High Minister explained the Crystal's origins to the Adjudicator. Some of this was news to him, too.

The Darksmith Collective was given a commission, Drakon explained. It was hired to do a job. And the Darksmith to whom that job was entrusted was Brother Varlos. Drakon seemed reluctant to point out that Varlos was the greatest Darksmith who had ever lived, but reading between the lines this seemed quite clear.

Varlos fulfilled his mission, but failed to pass on his invention to the Darksmiths or their clients. The Eternity Crystal was an important part – the most important part – of his project. The project belonged to the Darksmith Collective, therefore – so Drakon informed the court – the Crystal belonged to the Darksmith Collective. The Crystal had, however, been taken by the Doctor, who refused to return it to its rightful owners.

'Objection!' called the Doctor, cheerfully. 'It's not been proved that the Darksmiths are its rightful owners at all.'

'There is no question of proof!' shouted Drakon. 'Ownership of the Crystal is an indisputable fact!'

'It's not,' the Doctor told him, 'because I'm going to dispute it.'

A hiss of protest sounded around the court, as the Darksmiths realized the direction the Doctor's defence would take. The Doctor grinned around at them, as far as his bonds would let him. 'For example,' he said, 'what if I were one of the race who gave you this commission? The Crystal'd belong to me, then, wouldn't it?'

Drakon snarled at him. 'But you are not one of them.'

'Oh no?' said the Doctor. 'Gonna prove it? Who are they, then?'

Drakon gave him a superior smile. The Doctor grimaced; clearly the High Minister wasn't going to fall into such a simple trap. But it had been worth a shot. He really, really wanted to know who had commissioned the Darksmiths. Who had wanted, so badly, to resurrect the dead.

The Doctor had one last, half-hearted, attempt at pursuing this line: 'Look in my pocket,' he said, gesturing towards his jacket as well as he could. 'Look at my ID. I may not be of the race, but I think you'll find I'm their representative.'

The Adjudicator nodded at a Darksmith, who walked over to the Doctor, leant over him and pulled from his pocket the small wallet containing the psychic paper. He opened it, and gasped. 'Lord Drakon! He tells the truth! He is an agent of the K–'

Drakon cut across him. 'I do not believe it! I will not believe it!' He turned to the Adjudicator, almost spitting with rage. 'This is a trick!'

The Adjudicator gestured for the Darksmith to bring him the wallet. The Doctor held his breath. If this worked, he'd get the Crystal, the information, everything...

But it didn't work.

'A feeble attempt to fool the court,' the Adjudicator pronounced. 'Mere psychic trickery.'

'There's nothing "mere" about it,' the Doctor muttered, disappointed. He waved his fingers at the judge. 'May I have my psychic trickery back, then, please.'

Oh well. On to plan – what would it be by now? C? D? Getting nearer to Z, probably, by this point.

'The identity of the commissioners doesn't matter, anyway,' the Doctor said, brushing aside his previous argument, 'because it doesn't belong to them any more than it belongs to the Darksmith Collective. The Crystal belongs to just one Darksmith, the one who created it. Varlos.'

'But Varlos is dead!' cried Drakon.

'True,' agreed the Doctor. 'But by law – that is, the law of, ooh, I don't know, about a billion member planets and a million billion affiliated worlds – his property would then become the property of his heirs. That is to say, his nearest living relative.'

He turned to the Adjudicator, raising an eyebrow. The judge gave a solemn nod of agreement. 'That is correct. Unless the subject was party to a formal legal agreement by which any inventions-stroke-discoveries-stroke-creations automatically became the property of a direct employer, in this case the Darksmith Collective.'

The Doctor raised his other eyebrow at Drakon, who was staring in disbelief. 'Formal legal agreement?' cried the High Minister. 'He was part of the Collective, nothing more is required!'

The Doctor screwed up his face in mock sympathy. 'Ah, nothing signed, though. Silly, silly. Always get a contract, you can't trust anyone...'

Drakon waved a hand dismissively. 'All this is irrelevant. Varlos had no living relative.'

'You're wrong, you know.' The Doctor smiled.

On cue, with the sound of a thousand trumpeting elephants, the TARDIS appeared.

There were gasps from the Darksmiths as the TARDIS materialized on the dais in the centre of the courtroom. Even the Adjudicator seemed slightly taken aback.

The Doctor clicked his fingers, and the time ship's doors swung open. A young-looking, black-haired girl stepped through, gazing round the chamber with interest.

'Allow me to introduce Gisella,' the Doctor said. 'Varlos's daughter.'

Drakon was furious. 'Lies! Tricks!' he shouted. 'Varlos had no offspring!'

The Adjudicator was staring hard at Gisella – very hard. 'This humanoid is not of flesh and blood,' he announced. 'It is an android.'

That was a bit of a shock for the Doctor, who hadn't counted on anyone in the court having x-ray vision – or whatever extra-special sense had allowed the Adjudicator to work out the truth. But it didn't really affect what he had to say.

'Nevertheless,' he continued, addressing his remarks to the colourless man who was the Shadow Proclamation's representative, 'she is the daughter of Darksmith Varlos.'

'Nonsense!' interjected Drakon. 'Even if Varlos had crafted it with his own two hands, an android could no more be considered his daughter than a... a kettle!'

This pronouncement interested the Doctor immensely – not for any legal reasons, but because he had no idea that the Darksmiths were familiar with the concept of kettles. 'Ooh, I don't suppose there's any chance of a cuppa?' he asked, with what he hoped was a winning smile. 'Thirsty work, all this defending.' To his disappointment, both Drakon and the Adjudicator ignored him. Gisella gave him a grin, though. He winked back, then returned to the job in hand.

'Gisella,' the Doctor said, 'is a lot more than

just an android. And, by the way, Drakon, she's a "she", not an "it". Try to remember that, there's a good Darksmith.' He turned and looked directly at the Adjudicator. 'Gisella is an android, that's true – but she is also alive. Brought to life by the Eternity Crystal.'

Again, Drakos protested. 'Lies! All lies! The commission we were given was to bring life to things previously alive, to the dust and bones that had once been men. Varlos's device could no more give life to an android than it could to a... a...'

'Kettle?' suggested the Doctor. 'Toaster? Juicer? Food processor? Smoothie maker? Any other kitchen appliance? Sorry, where was I? Oh no,' he corrected himself, 'I should say, where were you? Telling me Varlos's machine couldn't actually create life, I think. Wrong!'

The Adjudicator leaned forwards. 'Doctor, creating truly sentient life through mechanical means has never been done. There are no reports from any planet in the system.'

The Doctor screwed up his face. 'Yeah, well, gotta be a first time for everything. And it's hardly likely Varlos was going to send a report in. After all, when he realized what he'd managed, he did everything he could to destroy the device! Mind you, between you and me –' He leant towards the Adjudicator and whispered out of the side of his mouth – 'I don't think anyone but Varlos could do it anyway, even with the device. Bit of extra-special Varlos magic – shall we call it magic? Not as if magic exists, but I'd have to invent a whole new word to explain it and no one except me would understand if I started running on about, I don't know, "flobbledobble" or something – anyway, bit of extra-special Varlos flobbledobble – no, let's stick with magic – bit of extra-special Varlos magic, and pfff! Life. Anyone else – abracadabra, izzy whizzy, still a kettle. Or toaster. Or smoothie maker. Or – excuse me, Gisella – an android.'

Gisella smiled at him. A seat had formed itself out of the dais for her, and she was sitting watching the Doctor with an indulgent look on her face, like a dog owner whose pet had just performed a clever trick. The Doctor had expected her to be, if not scared, then at least nervous about meeting what were essentially her evil in-laws, but she appeared to be taking it all in her stride. He took a deep breath.

'To conclude, Shadowy sir, Gisella's components

were fashioned by Varlos, and life was breathed into them by a device he created. I submit to the court that she is, in every sense both real and legal, and as Varlos himself proclaimed, his daughter, child, progeny or offspring, and therefore his heir.'

'And I submit to the court that this claim is ridiculous!' Drakon cried, but the Adjudicator was already nodding at the Doctor.

'Indeed,' the Adjudicator said, and the Doctor cheered inside. 'If what you say is true... If. It will need to be proved to the court.'

'Oh,' said the Doctor, his internal hurrahs subsiding. 'Er, I guess we could do that. Bit of time travel, get a few witness statements...'

But now the Adjudicator was shaking his head. 'I mean it must be proved that this child is the thing you claim: a living android. She will have to be taken apart.'

Drakon smiled. The Doctor gaped.

And suddenly Gisella didn't look so calm any more.

# Victory – and Defeat

**O**n occasions, the Doctor had had to hang around for decades, even centuries, waiting for things to happen. The hours that Gisella were gone seemed longer than any of them.

The bonds holding his arms had been absorbed back into the chair now the court was no longer in session, but his legs were still held tight. He stood up and sat down a few times, waved his arms around like twin windmills and then touched his toes, ignoring the few Darksmiths who had remained on the benches and were staring at him with disapproval. None of them had offered to get him a cup of tea.

At long last, the rest of the Darksmiths filed back into the chamber. Gisella followed, flanked by a pair of two Darksmith guards, then finally the Adjudicator came into the room. He and Gisella resumed their seats on the dais, and the Doctor was hugely relieved to see that Gisella looked fine. He mouthed 'Are you OK?' to her, and she nodded with a smile.

He then realized that he hadn't seen Drakon return. He turned – no, the High Minister wasn't in his seat, and even though the Doctor twisted right round until his body was pointed the opposite way to his feet, he could see no sign of him. Was he preparing a victory speech? Or... could it be that he wouldn't show his face in defeat? The Doctor held his breath as the Adjudicator began to speak.

'The subject Gisella has been examined, and has been found to be a living being–'

'Yeeees!' shouted the Doctor, punching the air. The Adjudicator gave him a disapproving look, but the Doctor was fairly certain there was a ghost of a smile underneath.

'She has been found to be a living being, and therefore has a legitimate claim to be the heir of Varlos.'

'Oh yes,' said the Doctor under his breath, grinning. 'Go Gisella.'

'As the Eternity Crystal is not the property of the Darksmiths, their claim against the

Doctor for theft has no substance, and the case is therefore dismissed.'

'Oh yes!' the Doctor echoed. 'Go Doctor!'

'However...'

The Doctor stopped and frowned. He'd played out this scenario in his head in a number of ways, but a 'however' hadn't featured in any of them.

'However...' the Adjudicator continued, 'as the Eternity Crystal is the legal property of Gisella, daughter of Varlos, it has been pointed out to me by High Minister Drakon that the Crystal must pass into her possession now, so justice is seen to be done. I have accepted this argument. Doctor, you will fetch the Eternity Crystal and give it to Gisella, daughter of Varlos, before these witnesses.'

The Doctor was desperately trying to think of a response that wouldn't have him held up for contempt of court. Drakon was obviously trying to claw back victory from defeat; the Doctor would have bet his remaining regenerations that the Darksmith had a trick or two up his sleeve. He glanced at Gisella, hoping she would step in, tell the Adjudicator that such a gesture was unnecessary – but she just sat there smiling, obviously not realizing the problem. Anyway, the Adjudicator would probably insist that he handed over the Crystal whatever she said. For a lot of people, the Doctor reflected, it was more important that justice was seen to be done than that justice was *actually* done.

'Oh, all right then,' he said at last. He beckoned to Gisella. 'Come along, kiddo.'

Two Darksmiths stepped forward. 'The girl will remain here. There must be witnesses.'

The Doctor looked at the Adjudicator hopefully, but the lawgiver shook his head. Then he gestured, and the cuffs that had glued the Doctor's legs to the chair were sucked back. The chair itself began to dissolve into the floor, and the Doctor jumped up hurriedly. A Darksmith appeared on either side of him, and he was led the few steps to the TARDIS.

Gisella hadn't shut the doors behind her and a crack of blue-white light hit the chamber floor, banishing the orange glow where it fell. The Doctor walked along the line of light almost superstitiously, feeling irrationally that if his feet strayed back into the pool of orange then somehow he would be doomed, like a child avoiding the cracks in the pavement so as not to awake the ever-patient bears that lurk below, waiting to pounce.

He reached the TARDIS, breathing a sigh of relief as he stepped on to the ramp leading down into the main control room. Then he shook his head, trying to rid himself of the wave of foreboding. That wasn't like him at all.

The two Darksmith guards were standing at the TARDIS doors – making sure he didn't escape, he assumed. Not that they'd have much chance of stopping him if he decided to make a break for it, but he wasn't going to leave Gisella behind.

But at the moment, the main thing he had to worry about was finding the Eternity Crystal.

The Doctor and Gisella had been worried about people getting into the TARDIS and taking the stasis casket containing the Crystal, so the Doctor had gathered up a number of other boxes and hidden the casket among them. However, Gisella had then become concerned that they themselves would forget which box was the right one, so she and the Doctor had composed a key.

Looking at the collection of boxes, the Doctor found the piece of paper containing the key, and examined it closely.

# Activity

Dear Doctor,
You can't hit me in cricket.
I'm lower than Shakespeare's night.
I'm not a prime minister's house visited by Rose, or
the body you were in when you met her.
I'm not a prime number.

Hope you find me!
love
the Eternity Crystal's box

'Hmmm,' thought the Doctor, as he tried to decide between two boxes. 'Oh, of course! Two is a prime number, because it can only be divided by one and itself! That means...'

He picked up box number eight and opened it. Yes, there was the Eternity Crystal all right.

Looking back at the discarded caskets, he considered for a minute trying to pull a fast one, taking an empty box out into the courtroom. Or the fake copy of the Crystal that Varlos had made as part of his first experiments and given to the Doctor. But, no. They'd be sure to insist on seeing the Crystal, and maybe testing it in some way to make sure it was the real one.

Anyway, why was he being so paranoid? The Crystal was rightfully Gisella's now; Drakon was hardly going to shoot them down and grab it, not in front of a member of the Shadow Proclamation.

The Doctor walked back out of the TARDIS, holding the small casket in front of him. The two Darksmiths moved out of his way, and left the dais. Gisella was still smiling – oblivious of the Doctor's concerns, or just putting on a brave face? Perhaps she was just so relieved that the Darksmiths had put her back together in one piece that anything else seemed trivial. She reached out and took the box from him, and clicked open the lid.

There were gasps from around the chamber as the gently glowing, egg-shaped Crystal was revealed.

'Gisella, daughter of Varlos,' said the Adjudicator, 'this Crystal is your rightful and legal property. Let no one take it from you.'

Apart from the Adjudicator, only the Doctor and Gisella remained on the central dais. Drakon's seat was still empty. So why was there so much tension in the air? Why did the Doctor feel barely able to take in a breath?

'There we go,' he said at last, forcing himself to speak normally. 'One Crystal, all yours. So, we'll be off then.'

He took a step back towards the TARDIS, expecting Gisella to follow him.

She didn't. A hooded Darksmith rose from the nearby benches and moved to stand at her side. 'No!' shouted the Doctor as he realized what was happening, as the Darksmith reached out gelatinous fingers and pulled the casket from Gisella's unresisting hands.

He suddenly found himself surrounded by swiftly moving Darksmiths, blocking his path in all directions. The Darksmith by Gisella, still clasping the box in one bony hand, used his other hand to pull back the heavy cowl covering his head.

Drakon.

'Thank you, Doctor,' said the High Minister. 'We will now proceed to hand over the Crystal and the device to our clients. It is thanks to you that we shall be able to fulfil this commission, and retain our one hundred per cent record.'

The Doctor gaped at him, and then turned to the Adjudicator. 'Aren't you going to say anything?' he cried. 'They're flouting your judgement right in front of you!'

'Not so,' Drakon interrupted. 'We have not taken the Crystal from this "daughter of Varlos" – she has given it to us freely.'

'Oh, Gisella,' said the Doctor sadly, realizing too late that something was very wrong with his friend, 'what have they done to you?'

'I have been fixed,' said the girl, still smiling. 'I no longer see things the wrong way. I understand that my future lies with the Darksmiths, and they should have the Eternity Crystal.'

# London and Dungeon

The Doctor again appealed desperately to the Adjudicator. 'They've reprogrammed her! That must be against some law or other, they were given permission to examine her, that was all!'

'But Gisella herself gave us permission to reprogramme her,' countered Drakon, his skull grinning more than ever beneath his rotten-jelly skin. 'And as this court has concluded that she is a living being, her words must be accepted.'

The Doctor boggled at him. 'I don't believe for a mili-micro-pico-second that Gisella gave you permission to alter her brain!'

'I did, Doctor,' the girl put in.

'Yeah, but you would say that – they've programmed you to!' The Doctor flung up his hands. 'There's not a single reason in the universe that would make someone volunteer to have their mind fiddled with like that!'

Gisella shook her head, still with that beatific smile on her face. 'You're wrong, Doctor. Drakon made me see how my place was here, with the Darksmiths. They are my own people, my only hope for a family. I choose to be with them, and I choose to help them fulfil their commission – I shall journey with them this very day to Galactic Reference 297-stroke-197AHG, where both the device, complete with Crystal, will be handed over to the Darksmiths' clients.'

Drakon had taken a step forwards during Gisella's speech, not quite going as far as to put a hand over her mouth, but perhaps in a vain hope that in getting between her and the Doctor, he could somehow prevent her words from reaching the Time Lord. She might be siding with the Darksmiths, thought the Doctor, but it seemed she hadn't yet learned their secrecy or guile.

He had one last try, turning again to the Adjudicator: 'Gisella would never have given permission for the Darksmiths to reprogramme her.'

The Adjudicator shook his head. 'As Gisella, daughter of Varlos, contradicts you and you have no other witnesses, there is no legal basis for a challenge.'

Drakon gazed at the Doctor in triumph. The Darksmiths surrounding the Time Lord stepped forward menacingly.

But just as they raised their skeletal hands, the Adjudicator spoke again. 'However, the Darksmiths have no authority to restrain the Doctor!'

The Doctor didn't wait another second. While the Darksmiths were assessing this, he ducked under their outstretched arms, and ran into the TARDIS, throwing a cheerful 'Thanks, your Shadowship!' behind him.

The TARDIS doors slammed shut, and the Doctor breathed a sigh of mingled relief and disappointment. He'd lost Gisella, he'd lost the Crystal. But he was free – and he was the Doctor! He'd get them both back, somehow.

Thanks to Gisella's careless talk, he knew exactly where to look. How best to go about it, though? The Darksmiths would surely be expecting him. The Doctor didn't think they'd be able to change the location of the meeting – there was probably a good reason for the clients to choose that particular place.

But there was one thing the Doctor had that the Darksmiths didn't – time travel. If he arrived just a little bit ahead of them – scout about, get out the binoculars and watch the skies in case a load of aliens dropped through – well, he wouldn't be quite so much on the back foot.

He moved over to the central console, and set the co-ordinates for Galactic Reference 297/197AHG. Perhaps he shouldn't have been surprised when he realized where he was heading, but nevertheless he was.

Why would the Darksmiths' clients have arranged the meeting on Earth?

The first thing the Doctor saw when he opened the TARDIS doors was a rock star looking at him. He did a quick double take, realizing he was facing a wall and the snarling, staring singer was gazing out of a poster.

'Aw, Jason Dungeon!' cried the Doctor. 'Brilliant!' A strip plastered across the top of the poster read 'Tonight!' The Doctor glanced at his wrist, even though he wasn't wearing a watch. The Darksmiths wouldn't arrive until tomorrow at the earliest, time for a quick concert before saving the world...?

Reluctantly, the Doctor decided he'd better not. He had to be alert, try to find out exactly where the meeting was going to take place, and maybe even come up with some sort of plan...

Gisella's co-ordinates had narrowed down the spot to about a square mile. That was better than having to search the whole galaxy – but it was still a fair distance to cover. He'd set up the sonic screwdriver to detect whenever something of significant size approached Earth's atmosphere, so he should be alerted when either the Darksmiths or their clients were getting near.

# TARDIS

## Data Bank

# Earth's Atmosphere

The atmosphere is a layer that surrounds Earth, protecting it from solar and cosmic radiation, extremes of temperature and meteors. The atmosphere consists of 78% nitrogen, 21% oxygen and 1% other gases, including argon, methane, neon, helium, hydrogen and carbon dioxide. Carbon dioxide is a 'greenhouse gas', which means it lets sunlight through to warm the planet, but does not let heat escape. The more carbon dioxide there is in the atmosphere, the hotter Earth will get!

Earth's atmosphere doesn't have a definite boundary, it gradually ceases to be. In the furthest part of the atmosphere there is so little gas it is almost a vacuum (*see TARDIS DATABANK: VACUUM). The outer area is called the exosphere, which, with the ionosphere, makes up the thermosphere. Below the thermosphere comes the mesosphere, then the stratosphere and finally the troposphere, which reaches to Earth's surface. The stratosphere contains the ozone layer, which blocks ultraviolet radiation from the sun. Some chemicals used on Earth can create holes in the ozone layer, meaning that harmful radiation could get through.

EXOSPHERE

THERMOSPHERE

IONOSPHERE

MESOSPHERE                                    500km

                                              80km

STRATOSPHERE

                                              50km

TROPOSPHERE

                                              15km

                                              0km

The Darksmiths and their clients would probably both be cloaked, but that wouldn't affect the size of their ships. A big spacecraft would need a big landing spot. And here – the Doctor looked around again, noting the venue name on the Jason Dungeon poster – yes, he'd thought so, he was in London, not well known for its wide open spaces.

Full of people, though, people he didn't want to get caught up in any alien fallout. People he didn't want to get hurt.

Suddenly, there was a crash and a scream.

People got hurt whether he wanted them to or not.

The Doctor was running before the crowds of humans seemed aware of the noise. He got to the scene as they began to gather, no one doing anything, just staring. A young girl lay in the road, not moving, her head tilted sideways with long dark hair hanging across her face. A man was climbing out of the black cab that had knocked her down, scared and blustering at the same time. 'She just ran out! I didn't see her! Didn't give me a chance!'

'Just ran out!' echoed a voice from the crowd. 'I saw it. Sounded like she was crying.'

'Reckon she had a row with her boyfriend or something,' added another. 'Just ran out, not thinking.

Kids of today, no consideration for others...'

The Doctor pushed through the gaping, speculating crowd and knelt down by the girl. He was relieved to see that her chest was rising and falling: she was still breathing, at least. Gently, so gently, careful not to move her even a millimetre, he brushed the hair off her face.

'I just didn't see her! I couldn't have seen her!' the cab driver was still saying.

'No,' said the Doctor, carefully. 'I don't think she could see you either.'

The driver stopped gabbling. 'What, you saying she's blind?'

'I think she must be,' said the Doctor, nodding. He looked down again at the girl's face. A face with blank skin where its eyes should be.

The girl's handbag was lying by her side. The Doctor opened it, and pulled out a large leather purse. Inside was a driver's licence. A driver's licence for a blind girl? No. The person in the picture was looking straight ahead, gazing with dark blue, long-lashed eyes. But it was undoubtedly the same girl who was lying unconscious on the road. A name was there too: Mae Harrison.

The crowd backed off as an ambulance drew

49

up, summoned by some passerby's mobile phone. A police car followed.

The Doctor wasn't allowed in the ambulance, despite backing up his claims of being a medical man with psychic-paper evidence. The police got the traffic moving again as the ambulance drove off, and the Doctor retreated, frowning, to the pavement.

He felt a tug on his sleeve.

Turning, he found a short, stocky bald man at his elbow. The man was dressed in a suit with a flashy red and yellow tie, and looked anxious. 'Did I hear you say you were a doctor?' he said.

The Doctor grimaced. Helping at an accident was one thing, a stranger wanting advice on a dodgy knee or a headache was another. But the man didn't wait for a reply before carrying on, talking at top speed. 'I didn't know what to do, it didn't seem like a medical thing, not something for a doctor, didn't want the papers to get hold of it, internet rumours, panic among the fans, but with the gig tonight...'

'Gig?' asked the Doctor, suddenly a bit more interested.

'He's got to do a concert tonight, sell-out, big tour, but I don't know how he's going to go on, can't see that it's something for a doctor but if someone could just look at him – if you could just look at him...'

'Look at who?' said the Doctor, thinking he already knew the answer.

The man looked from side to side, then leaned forward and whispered urgently. 'Jason Dungeon!'

The Doctor grinned. 'Really? Well, then, the Doctor will see him now!'

# The Lost Soul

The flustered man introduced himself as Jason's manager, Bill B. Brooks. His mobile phone went off five times as he led the Doctor into the theatre and to Jason's dressing room, but he barely glanced at it before cancelling each call. 'I don't know what to say to anyone!' he complained.

The Doctor still hadn't succeeded in finding out what the problem was by the time they reached the singer. And indeed, at first glance there didn't seem to be anything wrong with the man at all. He was sitting on a chair in the corner of his dressing room, watching a game show on a small television. He was dressed in lime-green trousers and an orange shirt, and his expression – what could be seen of it below a lime-green fedora – was serious, but not worried.

The Doctor looked at the singer, then at Bill B. Brooks. 'He seems fine,' he said.

Jason Dungeon turned away from the television and addressed the Doctor. 'I am fine,' he said. 'I do not know why people are in any way concerned. My head is fine. My neck is fine. My arms are fine. My chest is fine. My stomach is fine. My –'

'Yes yes yes,' interrupted the Doctor, realizing that perhaps his judgement had been a little too hasty. 'I'm sure there's nothing wrong at all with any of your body parts. It's just...' He turned to Bill B. Brooks, lost for words. 'It's just... he doesn't seem like this on the telly. Is he usually like this?'

'No!' The word almost exploded out of the manager. 'Wrecking hotel rooms, demanding this, that and the other, throwing tantrums – that's what he's usually like! I've never seen him so... quiet. So... so like he's not there any more.' He thought for a second. 'Let me demonstrate.' He picked up a disk and slotted it into a machine beneath the television. The game show cut out, replaced by a black screen, but Jason seemed unconcerned. A second later, a picture of Jason himself flashed up. He was mid-performance, singing a song the Doctor recognized as his worldwide hit *Never Love a Vampire*.

'Never love a vampire!' screeched the screen Jason, slashing a hand across his guitar and sliding across the stage on his knees.

Brooks turned to the real-life singer, who was watching the performance with only the faintest of interest. 'Jason, show the Doctor what you can do,' he said, as though talking to a reluctant toddler. 'Imagine you're on stage, sing along.'

'Never love a vampire!' screamed Jason on TV. 'Cos she might have a sweet tooth for her sweetheart!'

'For. Her. Sweet. Heart,' droned real Jason in a monotone, lagging some way behind.

'Oh dear,' said the Doctor.

'He's been like this for over an hour!' Bill B. Brooks told the Doctor, almost crying.

'Are you perhaps having a little joke with us, Mr Dungeon?' the Doctor asked. Jason stopped reciting the lyrics for a moment and shook his head.

'I don't think in this state he even understands what a joke is!' cried Brooks.

The Doctor had moved over to the singer. He took Jason's chin in his hand, and stared straight into his eyes. When the Doctor turned back to Bill, his own eyes held a worry that had not been there before.

'What did he do earlier?' the Doctor asked. 'Back when he was... normal.'

Bill shrugged. 'Nothing major,' he said. 'Just an interview for a magazine this morning. That was all...'

The Doctor kissed his psychic paper after it came in useful for the millionth time, this time getting him into the offices of *Hi There!* magazine, where he spoke to writer Shelley Sayers. 'Yeah, I spoke to Jason Dungeon this morning,' she said, taking a long slurp of a milkshake. 'What, ill? No, seemed OK to me. Bit cheeky, you know what these rock stars are like. I'm just writing it up now – last minute thing, we go to press this afternoon.'

'Was there anyone else there with you?' asked the Doctor, fishing for any information at all.

She shook her head. 'Nope, just me and Jason.' She grinned. 'Used to be exciting, one on one with the stars. Just another day at the office, now. I'm getting old.'

'Yes,' said the Doctor, not noticing her flash of disappointment as he agreed with her. 'Look, can I read the article? Please?' There could be clues there, things that someone with a nose for trouble might be able to spot.

Shelley screwed up her face, then had to push

her glasses back up her nose. 'Not now,' she said. 'Work in progress. Tell you what, pop back in an hour or so and I'll do you a printout.' She gave a final slurp, and the last dregs of milkshake rattled up her straw. 'Now, if you'll excuse me...'

The Doctor thanked her, and left. He wasn't any further on. But he had to find out what was happening.

He had to discover who had stolen Jason Dungeon's soul.

The Doctor knew he should be concentrating on locating where the Darksmiths' rendezvous would take place. It could affect so many thousands of people – but right here, right now, there were two people who definitely needed his help.

He made his way to the hospital where Mae Harrison had been taken. But she was still unconscious, and no one was allowed to see her – even such a 'distinguished surgeon' as the harassed receptionist soon believed the Doctor to be. He could probably have found a way to get in – but if the girl wasn't talking, there wouldn't be a lot more he could discover. Feeling frustrated, he hopped on a bus and returned to the magazine offices.

Back at *Hi There!* the Doctor found that Shelley Sayers was out having a very late lunch, but he was pleasantly surprised to discover she'd remembered his request and left a printout of the article with a colleague. It wasn't just her text – it was a mock-up of how the feature would appear in the magazine, complete with a picture of Jason, sneering from beneath the brim of his hat: full of life, full of personality.

The Doctor read quickly through the article. Then he sighed, and crumpled the paper into a ball. Nothing, nothing he could see that was relevant at all; nothing to show how this person so full of life had become the bland non-entity he'd met in the dressing room...

The Doctor blinked. He hurriedly unwrapped the ball of paper, flattening it out as best as he could. He should have spotted it before: the Jason in the photo and the Jason that he'd met were wearing exactly the same clothes. Green trousers, green fedora. Orange shirt.

He hurried over to the man who'd given him the printout. 'This picture! Was it taken today?'

The man shrugged. 'Maybe. We usually get new photos to go with articles. You could ask at the picture desk.' He gestured over to the other side of the office.

The Doctor darted over there, repeating his question. Yes, the photo had been taken today. 'But Shelley said she was on her own in the interview,' the Doctor said. 'Did she take the picture herself?'

No, she wouldn't have done that. They'd sent along a photographer.

'Can you tell me who it was?' the Doctor asked, adding, 'Please please please pretty please?'

The picture editor shrugged. 'Don't see why not, the credit'll be in the mag.' He tapped at his keyboard, locating a file. 'There. Des Martin.'

'Know him?' said the Doctor.

The man nodded. 'Yeah, one of our regulars. Good guy.'

The Doctor frowned, wondering how to phrase a question asking if this Des Martin had ever shown any signs of being a soul-stealing alien and/or supervillain – but before he could open his mouth again, a woman leant across the picture disk and said, 'Hang on – I thought Shelley said a woman turned up to do the shots.'

'Really?' The Doctor turned and gave her a beaming smile. 'And did she say anything else?'

But the woman shook her head. 'Just warned me

that the pictures might not be up to scratch, as Des didn't take them. But they're fine.'

The Doctor took a deep breath. 'And no one knows who this mysterious female photographer from out of nowhere might be?'

Everyone shook their heads.

'So does anyone know where Shelley Sayers has gone for lunch?'

Everyone shook their heads again.

'She'll probably be back in half an hour,' said someone. But the Doctor didn't want to wait another half an hour. He'd already wasted enough time. He knew he was getting close, just knew – but every second might count.

Then he remembered the milkshake she had been drinking. It was a chance, just a tiny chance, but people often went back to the same places again and again... He dashed over to Shelley's desk, scrabbled in her bin – to the horror of the rest of the writers – and came up with the empty cardboard container. 'Where's this?' he asked, pointing at the fast-food logo on the cup. A man at the next desk told him, and the Doctor ran off out of the office, a host of bemused stares following his progress.

# Natasha's Story

**H**e grinned as he entered the restaurant. Sitting at a booth near the door, a paperback in one hand and a bunch of fries in the other, was Shelley Sayers.

'Ooh, give us one of those,' said the Doctor, plumping himself down on the uncomfortable plastic bench opposite her.

'Say please,' she replied, pushing the tray over to him. The Doctor helped himself to a fry, and thanked her profusely.

'Never used to be much of a chip man, but I had this friend...' he told the writer. 'Can't resist 'em now.'

She looked him up and down. 'You'd never guess,' she said. 'Mr Skinny.'

The Doctor waved that away, because he wasn't quite sure if she meant it as a compliment or an insult. He put the printout on the table, smoothing it out further. 'Who took the picture?' he said, putting a finger on Jason Dungeon's printed nose.

'Oh, some woman,' Shelley replied. 'It was supposed to be this guy, Des Martin, but she turned up instead. Said he was away and she was covering for him. Don't think I ever heard her name, but she'd got all the gear, appeared to know what she was doing and Jason was happy, so no skin off my nose.'

'And you didn't notice anything odd about her?'

The writer shook her head. Then she frowned. 'Well... not really. She was just a bit... oh, I don't know how to describe it.'

'Go on, have a go,' nudged the Doctor.

'Well – a bit off in fairyland, I suppose. Just a hint that she was sort of – absent. But nothing I could really put my finger on.'

The Doctor thought back to Jason Dungeon. 'Absent. You know, I have a feeling you might have just given me a very good description indeed.' He took a deep breath. 'OK, now for the big one. Do you know where I can find her?'

Shelley shrugged. 'Sorry, no idea. You could ask Des Martin, I guess. What's all the fuss about? I can recommend loads of good photographers if you want some shots taken. This one wasn't anything special – although I suppose she was a bit of a looker, if you care about that sort of thing. Blonde hair, big blue eyes...' Her expression made it clear that she didn't care about that sort of thing, and she hoped that no one she met would either.

The Doctor asked her for Des Martin's phone number. He then borrowed her mobile to ring it. No answer.

'Well, there wouldn't be, if he's away,' Shelley commented.

The Doctor felt a bit hopeless as he left the restaurant. He pulled his sonic screwdriver out of his pocket and looked at it, half-hoping it would sound the alarm, give him a proper big alien battle to get his teeth into. But he knew he couldn't really walk away and leave this mystery. Missing eyes, missing personality. Not an everyday state of affairs.

He'd got the address of Des Martin's studio from Shelley. So the guy wasn't there, but a bit of sonicking and he might pick up some details of this mysterious blonde photographer – notes by the phone, business card on the desk, anything like that.

The studio was only a few tube stops away. The Doctor took a short cut to the station via a residential street, stuffed full of old Victorian houses, each one now probably divided into a lot of tiny flats judging by the number of doorbells.

He was nearly at the tube station when he heard crying. Something in the sound thudded into his head like an arrow: this was the wild, exhausted cry of a human in unnatural distress.

It seemed to be coming from below him, almost under his feet. He looked down – yes, there was a basement window, and steps beside him led down to a door that was lower than the street. He hurried down the staircase and put his head against the window. He couldn't see anything – curtains were drawn inside – but he'd been right, this was where the sobbing came from: hopeless, ceaseless sobbing.

He knocked on the window. 'Hello?'

The sobs paused – 'Go away!' – then began again.

'I'm a Doctor,' the Doctor called. 'Let me help you.'

No answer.

'Stay there, then,' he said. 'I'm coming in anyway.'

A few sonics later, and the Doctor was stepping

into the basement flat. He made his way down a short hallway into a dark living room. Not much natural light would have made its way into a place this low down anyway; with the curtains drawn it didn't stand a chance. But he could make out the shape of a woman sitting in a chair. Her head was turned away from the Doctor and she was clearly crying, but still, something didn't seem right about the profile she was presenting. Well – not if she were human.

'Look at me,' the Doctor said.

Almost as if hypnotised, she turned to face him.

It might have looked funny, in other circumstances. A child's drawing with a feature forgotten. For the Doctor, so used to beings of all shapes and sizes and appearances, it scarcely registered as strange. But it was strange. Where the woman should have had a nose, there was just blank skin. No holes, no scars, no lumps of flesh, just smoothness.

The Doctor crouched down beside the girl, and took hold of a trembling hand. 'What's your name?' he asked her.

She didn't stop crying, but whispered, 'Datasha.'

'Well, Datasha...'

'Doh! Datasha!'

'I'm sorry.' The Doctor gripped her hand tighter, and spoke slowly and calmly to her, as if to an upset toddler. 'Well, Natasha, I'm the Doctor. I'm not an ordinary doctor, I'm a special doctor. I sort out things like this.'

She looked up, desperate hope surging into her eyes. 'You cab hepp be?'

'Yes, I can help you.' He tried to sound confident. After all, he had more chance of helping her than anyone else on the planet, even if at that moment he didn't quite know how. 'Tell me what happened to you. Who did it?'

Her sobs were dying down now, the Doctor proving a comforting presence. Her eyes were wide as she began her story – not that there was much of a story to tell. It all happened so quickly.

It had been the night before. Natasha had had a feeling she'd been followed on the way home, but had dismissed it once she was back at her flat, safe. Her boyfriend had visited, they'd eaten pasta and drunk wine and then he'd left. It had started raining a few minutes later: that pulsing, pounding rain that bruises as it hits the skin.

She'd thought the knock on the door had been her boyfriend, seeking shelter before venturing out again. But it was a woman. Her soaking wet hair straggled across her face, so it was a moment before Natasha realized what was so odd about her. And then, before she could react further, Natasha was asleep. When she awoke, she discovered...

'It's all right,' the Doctor said hurriedly.

'Ad I'b tried ad tried to call Nes but he's dot dere!'

'Who's Nes?' asked the Doctor, still interpreting.

'Dot Nes! *Nes!* By boyfrieb!'

'Oh, Des!' Then the Doctor stopped. 'Not Des Martin?'

'Do you doh hib?'

'No,' said the Doctor. 'But things are starting to all tie up somehow. I just need to find out how. And why. And, er, who.'

He tried Des Martin's number again, but there was still no answer. The Doctor was beginning to have a bad feeling about that.

'You woulderd dink it, but I'b a bodel,' Natasha told him. 'Dat's how I bet Nes.'

The Doctor was quite anxious to meet Des himself. So, with a final promise that he really would sort out everything, he set off on his way again.

Fifteen minutes later he was opening the door to Des Martin's studio. It was gloriously filled with white sunlight, and the Doctor wondered how someone could bear to hide away in Natasha's dim flat after experiencing this. One end of the studio was blank and empty, ready to be filled with photographic subjects, the other acted as an office, and had walls plastered with prints.

The Doctor spotted various celebrities – as well as many, many faces he didn't know, but who would probably call themselves celebrities too. Fleeting fame often passed a Time Lord by; it was easy to overlook seconds when there were centuries to watch. Natasha was on the wall in shot after shot, her full-featured face striking.

Standing there, gazing at the faces on the wall, the Doctor suddenly had the feeling that he was not alone in the room.

'Hello?' he called cheerfully. There was no reply.

He listened carefully. Yes – there was the sound of someone breathing, steadily and calmly.

'Hello?' he tried again. Still nothing.

To one side of the room, between the blankness and the office, there stood a number of painted Chinese screens, perhaps providing a shield for quick changes of clothes. The Doctor crept towards them. With a sudden 'aha!' he pulled back a screen.

The man standing behind it looked at the Doctor with no particular interest.

'Hello,' said the Doctor.

'Hello,' said the man.

'Are you Des?'

'Yes I am Des.'

'And are you all right, Des?'

'Yes I am all right.'

The Doctor turned away. He'd been worried about what he might find here: in many ways this was better than some of the things he'd imagined. Des was feeling no pain, no distress. But as far as the Doctor could tell, he was feeling nothing else either.

The Doctor picked up a camera from the top of a filing cabinet. Just an ordinary digital camera, point and click, nothing fancy. He handed it to Des.

'Do you know what this is?' he asked.

But Des the photographer looked as blank as the far studio wall.

# TARDIS
## Data Bank

# Photography

The English word 'photography' is taken from a Greek phrase meaning 'writing with light'. Early photos were created using pewter plates exposed to light, or metal plates covered with silver iodide, a chemical that is sensitive to light. Neither of these methods produced clear pictures.

The next form of photograph also used silver iodide, but involved a piece of equipment called a camera. The camera and the new process were invented by William Henry Fox Talbot in 1841. As the silver iodide that had been exposed to light turned black, but the remainder did not, an image was created that was the exact opposite of the photographed scene. This image — with light parts shown black, and dark parts shown light — was called a negative. When light was shone through the negative, a black-and-white reproduction of the original scene could be made.

SUBJECT · NEGATIVE · PHOTOGRAPH

Film made of celluloid replaced the silver-iodide-coated plates or paper by the late nineteenth century, and cameras became smaller. With this new equipment, photography became much more common. Photography became a popular profession — and, by the 1920s, a popular hobby too.

Digital photography has returned to using light-sensitive plates instead of film — but uses electronic circuits to convert the information stored on the plate into code, which is then stored on a computer chip.

# Trading Places

**H**aving sat Des on a chair, the Doctor started looking for clues. An address book was full of names, bulging with bits of paper and business cards pushed in at the appropriate pages, but he didn't think any of that would help.

There was a diary, though. The Doctor turned to the right page. Morning: Jason Dungeon. Then in the afternoon, the single phrase 'Market Square'. If this mysterious woman was keeping Des's appointments for him, perhaps that's where she could be found. But there was no further clue – no house number, no town name. A quick flick through Des's address book revealed no one who lived in a market square. The Doctor's only hope was that it was local.

He left the studio and looked around him,

hopelessly hoping to see a big sign saying 'Market Square this way'. There wasn't, of course, but he spied a newsagent's shop instead and popped inside.

He gave the elderly woman behind the counter one of his most charming grins. 'Sorry to bother you,' he said, 'but can you tell me if there's a market square nearby?'

She frowned at him. 'Market? There's no market around here. There's the square with the statue of the man in it, if that's what you're wanting.'

The Doctor suspected it wasn't, but obtained directions anyway. 'But it's definitely not called "Market Square"?' he confirmed.

'What, like off the telly? No.'

The Doctor was halfway through the door when this registered. He backed up. '"Off the telly"?'

'You know, the soap.'

'Actually,' the Doctor told her, 'I don't know.'

She gestured behind him. He turned to find a rack stuffed full of magazines, and when he plucked out the nearest one he saw it had 'Market Square: Now Four Nights a Week!' written on the cover. He flicked through it, spotting the name 'Des Martin' as a credit under several pictures.

'It's a soap opera!' he realized.

The shopkeeper didn't know where the soap was filmed, apart from that it was somewhere in London, but was extremely happy to sell the Doctor copies of *Market Square Monthly*, *Inside Telly*, *Television Show Times* and *Soap Choice*. The Doctor sat on a bench outside and read them all in forty-five seconds, learning a lot about the everyday lives of supposedly ordinary folk, many of them Australian. He also tried to pick up every scrap of information that might help him discover where *Market Square* was filmed...

# Activity

Four possible locations for Market Square:

Vienna Studios
Lakeview Studios
Tulip Studios
Television Towers

Clues:

'Market Square' used to be filmed in a huge converted warehouse, but the soap moved six months ago to its current location when the building was condemned as unsafe.

'Market Square' star Deirdre Dunlop preferred it when the soap was filmed at the Vienna Studios, as she lived almost next door.

The Tulip Studios have only been open for three months.

When Little Mikey's boating adventure was filmed, the crew had to travel several miles as there was no body of water near the studio.

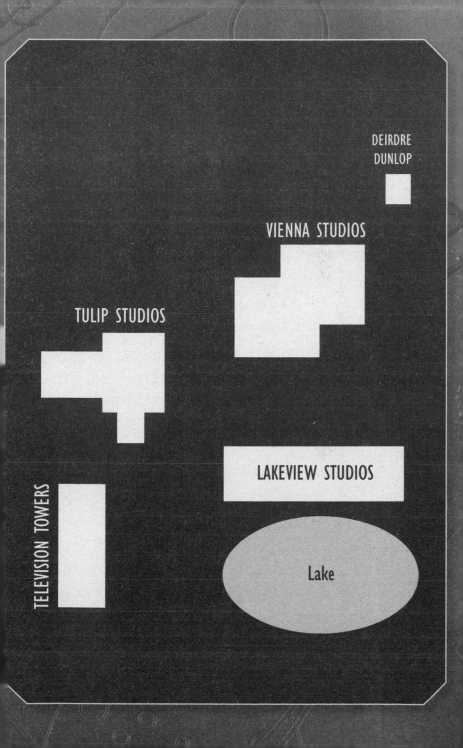

'Let's hope "Lakeview" is an accurate name,' commented the Doctor, as he crossed his fingers and consulted a map to find the location of Television Towers.

The Doctor weaved through the corridors of Television Towers, holding his psychic paper in front of him like a talisman. Anyone who glanced at it saw some form of document that said the Doctor had a perfect right to be wherever he was.

A stressed-looking woman with a clipboard hurried past the Doctor, her eyes darting towards the psychic paper as she went. He had already taken a couple more steps forward when he felt a hand grabbing at his arm. The woman had turned round and was staring at him as if he were the answer to her prayers.

'At last!' She looked him up and down. 'Yes, you'll do. Come with me, quickly!'

The Doctor allowed himself to be hustled down the corridor. 'Er, where are we going?'

'Hair and makeup. Nothing drastic, I don't think, just spike the hair up a bit more, bit of gel, that should do it.' She looked at him critically. 'But then wardrobe, definitely. I mean, what were you thinking? A market trader in a suit? Shoes are OK, we'll keep the shoes, but jeans and a T-shirt is what we're looking for. Didn't the agency tell you?'

'No, they didn't,' the Doctor said with complete honesty. 'You know, I'm not sure I'm right for this part.'

'Nonsense!' The woman was walking even faster now. 'Anyway, you couldn't be worse than the one we've got there now. Can't say a single line!'

'Really? Not one?'

'Not one. You'd think he'd never even spoken before, let alone acted.' The woman tutted loudly at the horror of people who couldn't even act.

The Doctor, who had been trying to extricate himself from the woman's grasp, finally allowed himself to be led along without fuss. It sounded like he'd come to the right place after all.

The Doctor had fun in wardrobe, choosing blue jeans and a red T-shirt. He tried to persuade the girl there, Megan, to let him wear an admiral's hat that he'd spotted – but although she seemed inclined to be indulgent towards him, she reluctantly shook her head.

'Oh,' said the Doctor, disappointed. 'I've always wanted one of those. I thought it looked really dashing on Nelson. He wouldn't let me wear one either. "Doctor," he said, "I'm the admiral and I need my hat. If I let you borrow it all the sailors would get confused, and before you know it they'll be splicing the anchor and hauling in the main brace, and then where will we be?"'

Megan laughed the worried laugh of someone who didn't get the joke and thought it might be on her. She held out a battered bomber jacket, rather like a peace offering. 'I think this'd work.'

The Doctor agreed, and slipped it on. 'There.'

She sighed. 'Oh, you look ever so handsome,' she said. 'Have you done much telly?'

Again, the Doctor was able to answer truthfully that he had not.

'Oh, the camera's going to love you.' She leaned forward and whispered in confidence. 'Look, I know it's only a couple of lines. But you know Big Ned?'

'Mmm?' the Doctor replied, non-committally.

'He started off just in the market, only in for one scene, just like you. But he was so nice and charming they brought him back and let him do some more, and *then* they let him get into a fight with Dodgy Dave, and in the end he discovered Len robbing the King's Head and got into a big car chase and crashed off a bridge and died in an enormous explosion! So, if you play your cards right, that could happen to you!'

'Hurrah!' said the Doctor, trying to look pleased at the idea.

'It was in all the papers,' Megan said happily.

'I suppose there's a lot of that,' the Doctor said. 'Photographers coming round, snapping the cast...'

'Yes.' She nodded. 'I think there's one around at the moment, on the set.'

The Doctor adjusted his bomber jacket. 'Well, in that case it's probably about time I got to the set too, isn't it?'

# What a Picture

It looked just like a real market, except for the huge cameras and the lights. The woman with the clipboard – whose name turned out to be Pamela – was there, as well as about twenty other people, all looking equally stressed and busy.

All, that is, except one. A man sat on a fold-up chair to one side of the set, looking blankly into the distance and muttering to himself. The Doctor made his way over to him.

'Hello,' said the Doctor.

'Get your Granny Smiths,' replied the man. 'They are lovely. Two pounds of apples for one pound.'

Pamela with the clipboard approached. 'Don't worry about him,' she said to the Doctor. 'He hasn't got a clue. Security's going to chuck him out.'

'Is this the man I'm replacing?' the Doctor asked,

trying not to show in his voice the contempt he felt for her attitude.

'Uh-huh.' She gestured over to one of the mocked-up market stalls, covered with fruit and vegetables. 'Look, you stand next to that. Here's your line –' She adopted an exaggerated accent. '"Git chor Granny Smiffs! They're luvverly! Two pahnds of apples for a pahnd!" Got that?'

'I think so,' the Doctor replied.

'Right. Then you've just got to look busy in the background as George and Lovely Lucy come on arguing.'

'Look busy. OK,' said the Doctor. 'Incidentally,' he carried on, gesturing at the man whose role he'd taken, 'was this gentleman here when photos were being taken of the set?'

The woman sighed. 'Yes, worse luck. I mean, that's so annoying, because he's not going to appear in the show – so all the fans'll see the photos and come up with elaborate conspiracy theories as to why it's a different trader. We can hardly tell them that the bloke was just a useless pile of junk.'

'Mmm,' said the Doctor, biting his tongue again, and then deciding not to. 'Or that the bloke was taken ill on the set and you didn't even call a doctor. I mean, I bet he wasn't like this earlier. You probably thought he was going to be fine in the part. It was only after the photographer had finished snapping away that you noticed he was like this.' He pointed towards the poor actor, still staring and muttering on his chair.

Pamela sniffed. 'Look, do you want this part or not?'

'Do I get to have my photo taken? Is the photographer still here?'

She looked annoyed. 'Actors! Yes, the photographer's still here. She's shooting George and Lovely Lucy at the moment, but she'll be back in a bit.'

'Then yes,' said the Doctor. 'I want this part.'

A small man with a moustache and a loud voice called for action. The Doctor stood next to the fruit and veg stall, his thumbs in his belt, and shouted out enthusiastically about apples. Megan from wardrobe had come in to watch, and gave him a thumbs-up from the sidelines as a skinny girl with blonde hair and a bald-headed man walked out on to the set.

The blonde girl looked straight ahead, and said

levelly: 'Leave it out George. You are not my uncle and I am sure of it.'

'Yes I am your uncle, sweetheart,' droned the bald man in reply.

The moustached man, his eyes wide and incredulous, ran out on to the set, shouting 'Cut, cut!' He went up to the skinny girl and threw up his hands. 'No no no! Lucy, remember, you accused George of kidnapping your beloved kitten, the Fluffster, but he's just told you he's your long-lost step-uncle here to challenge Angela's will! It's a big deal! Put some emotion into it!'

'Leave it out George. You are not –'

'That's even worse! And for goodness' sake look at him, not at me!' The irate man gestured at 'George', who was staring at a point somewhere past the Doctor's fruit stall.

'Hello!' said the Doctor, stepping forward. 'I wonder if I can help.'

The man with the moustache stared at him. 'You? You're just an extra!'

'I'm not sure if that's technically true,' said the Doctor. 'I mean, I did have a line.' But seeing that the man was about to explode, he carried on: 'Actually, I'm not even ·an actor. You see what happened to these two? I know what it is. At least, I'm pretty sure. And I think I can sort it out. But I need to know one thing: where is the photographer?'

'What photographer?' screeched the man.

'Oh, female, blonde hair, blue eyes, maybe carrying a few loose souls under her arm...'

'*What?*'

'Er – do you mean her?' said clipboard Pam.

The Doctor looked. A tall, stunningly good-looking woman was walking towards him. She had a camera slung round her neck on a strap, and was staring enraptured at the Time Lord.

'So much inside...' she was murmuring. 'Oh, I must have it...' She raised the camera to her eye.

'I don't think so!' yelled the Doctor. 'Don't let her look you in the eyes!' he called out to the various actors and crew members who were watching this with some interest. 'And definitely don't look down the lens of her camera!'

There was a sudden whirring noise. 'Hey!' shouted one of the cameramen, perched on his platform, 'My camera's going all by itself!'

'So's mine!' called another.

Nearly everyone turned to look at the cameras, even as the Doctor cried out 'Don't look!'

It was too late. Even from this distance he could see the light leave every pair of eyes. The crew sank back, no longer animated, and the blonde photographer gave a whoop of triumph. The Doctor risked a quick glance – her eyes had rolled back in her head and she was breathing in deeply. Something seemed familiar to the Doctor, then he realized what it was – she reminded him of Shelley the journalist, sucking up her milkshake through a straw.

'What's happening?' came a scared voice from the edge of the set. The Doctor didn't dare look round. The cameras were all around the room, nowhere was safe. But he recognized the voice – it was Megan from wardrobe. Somehow, she'd managed to avoid the cameras' gaze.

'Megan!' called the Doctor. 'You've got to get out of here!'

'But all the people –'

'There's nothing you can do! She's linked all the cameras to her own one somehow, so you mustn't look into the lenses – I'm serious, not even a glance – and you've got to get away while she's otherwise engaged! I'll sort things out here!'

With his head bowed, the Doctor started to make his way towards the photographer. He reached into his pocket – if he could reverse whatever she'd done to the cameras, it would make his life a lot easier. He just needed his sonic screwdriver...

It wasn't there.

The Doctor's hand was in the pocket of his costume jeans, and the sonic screwdriver was still inside his coat.

'Megan!' he called again. 'Have you gone yet?'

To his relief, her voice came back: 'No!'

'Then I need you to do something for me. Fetch my clothes. My proper clothes. There's something very important in my coat pocket. Bring everything back here, but whatever you do, don't look at any cameras on your way. Got that?'

'Yes,' she replied, sounding nervous. A pause, and then, 'Who are you?'

'I'm the Doctor. And I need you to hurry!'

A few seconds later he heard a door bang, and sighed with relief. He kept going, working his way around various market stalls and their spilled contents, to get to the photographer. He nearly tripped over a rail of clothes, a felt-tipped sign fastened to the end proclaiming 'SALE! EVERYTHING £5'.

Suddenly a voice came from somewhere in front

of him. 'I need you. Come to me. Look at me.'

'No thanks,' said the Doctor. He picked up the clothes rail and pushed it in front of him like a lycra-and polyester-hung shield. 'You see, I think I know who you are.'

'Do you?'

'Oh yes. Mind you, here's a question: do *you*? You probably don't. You think you're a proper human,' the Doctor said. 'But you're not.'

# Caught on Camera

The woman gave a hiss of rage. 'I am human!'

'Are not,' the Doctor retorted. 'I expect you don't even have a name!'

'I do!'

'Well, what is it, then?'

There was a pause, then the voice said, slowly, 'My name is Mitra. Mitra Ashkanazi.'

'Is it, now? Well, if you say so. But that doesn't change the fact that you're really not a human.'

'Then what am I?'

Before the Doctor could answer, there came the sound of a door opening. 'Megan?'

'Yes, it's me. I've got –'

'Good,' the Doctor interrupted. He didn't want Mitra Ashkanazi to realize he had a sonic ace up his sleeve. Then he had another thought. The studio had no windows, relying instead on huge lighting units. And as far as he could see, Mitra's camera didn't even have a flash. If there was no light in the room... 'Megan, listen, can you find a way of turning off the lights? Then you'll be able to move more freely. And so will I,' he added to himself.

'OK,' Megan called back. 'But... Doctor, what is she?'

The Doctor smiled grimly to himself. 'Funny you should ask, I was just going to explain that very thing to her...' He pushed the clothes rail forward a few metres. 'Megan, let me introduce you to Mitra Ashkanazi. A Vacant.'

'A what?'

'A what?' echoed Mitra.

'A Vacant. A nothing.' He thought for a moment, and then said, 'You know cuckoos? How a cuckoo lays its egg in another bird's nest, and when the baby cuckoo hatches it kills the other fledglings and steals everything it needs to grow from its false family? Well, that's rather how Vacants operate. A Vacant starts life as a sort of blob in roughly humanoid form, and it's dumped on some poor unsuspecting planet. Like Earth.'

Suddenly the studio was plunged into darkness.

'Good girl, Megan!' the Doctor called. 'That should make things easier. Now, make your way towards me!' He was hoping that he was right, that if they couldn't see the cameras, the cameras couldn't see them...

'Do I look like a "rough humanoid" to you?' came Mitra's voice, responding to his explanation.

'No,' the Doctor replied, 'but that's my whole point. You see, once on a suitable planet, the Vacant starts taking everything it needs from the dominant species there – piece by piece. A leg here, an arm there – it puts its victims to sleep and removes the next thing on its list, leaving its own formless blobby bits in exchange. Heads, shoulders, knees and toes, eyes and ears and mouth and nose... And let's not go any further than that. It acts on instinct – the first thing it takes is a pair of eyes, then it can see what it's doing. It's attracted to pretty things, just like a small child – or a bird. That's why Vacants usually end up being quite striking by the standards of the planet they're on.'

'I don't understand,' said Megan, and the Doctor was pleased to hear that her voice sounded a lot nearer now. 'What's that got to do with what's happened here? All the people going blank?'

'Ah, well, that's the next stage. A Vacant really is empty, you see. So once they've built themselves a proper body, they start to absorb personality too.' He grimaced. 'That's why they're so hard to find. Usually, they slurp up a bit of dull Mr or Mrs Average, no ambition, quite content – and so they settle down happily, content themselves. But this time...'

He thought for a moment, working out exactly what must have happened.

'Somehow, we won't know how until she wakes up – and perhaps not even then – a girl called Mae Harrison stumbled across the Vacant. The Vacant put her to sleep and stole her eyes. When Mae woke up she ran out, scared and blind – past a lot of people who ignored her, incidentally – until she ran into the road and was knocked down by a cab. Then, armed with a pair of beautiful blue eyes, Mitra here starts gathering up all the other bits she needs – along with some clothes so she can blend into human society without attracting too much attention. Am I right so far?'

Mitra's voice sounded faintly puzzled. 'Perhaps.'

'Well, yes, you might not remember much of what happened back then. You were just operating on instinct. So I'll tell you what I think happened next. Let's assume that by last night you were complete except for a nose. You spot a young woman called Natasha – she's a model, not surprisingly your jackdaw instincts draw you to her, wanting a bit of that for yourself – and you follow her home. Something inside you knows that all this has to be done in secrecy or you might be creating danger for yourself, so you hold back when Natasha's boyfriend, Des, arrives. When he's gone, though, you carry on and do what you have to do – and the outside of your head is complete. But now you need something to fill the inside.'

There was a gagging sound from Megan. 'You mean she sucks out people's brains?'

'Not quite,' said the Doctor, hoping that the girl was going to reach him soon. He was fairly sure he wasn't far away from Mitra, but telling the Vacant her own story was keeping her distracted at the moment. If he could just hold her interest for long enough to get his sonic screwdriver and disable all the cameras...

'She doesn't take actual brains, although sucking isn't a bad description of how she fills her head. What she needs is their personality, their very being. "Soul" is probably the wrong word to use, but I think you understand what I mean by it. Now, this is only a guess, but as it's a guess by me it's pretty likely to be right: on her way out of the flat, she bumps into Natasha's boyfriend Des Martin, who's popping back to get out of the rain. Mitra here is pretty attractive and Des is a photographer. Perhaps he suggests taking photos of her. They go off to his studio.'

'And she zaps him with a magic camera?' Megan suggested. There was a crash as the girl tripped over something, probably a market stall. 'Ow!'

'You OK?'

'Yes. I think a pineapple fell on my head, though.'

The Doctor gave a short laugh. 'Could be worse. Do you know how many people are killed each year by falling coconuts?'

Megan snorted. 'I think standing under a dozen palm trees might be safer than where I am right now...'

'Oh yes,' agreed the Doctor. He recalled her earlier question and addressed the area where he thought Mitra was. 'You didn't have a camera then, though, did you, Mitra? It was Des Martin who had the camera. You just stared into it.'

He turned back in Megan's direction. 'You know

the saying "the eyes are the windows to the soul"? Well, the trouble is, burglars can get in through windows. That's what Vacants do. Stare into their eyes long enough and they can steal everything from you. They're like a vacuum, you see. Nothing in them, everything in you. Make a connection between you and the soul is pushed into the void.'

# TARDIS

## Data Bank

## Vacuum

The English word 'vacuum' is taken from the Latin word 'vacuus', meaning empty. A vacuum is an empty area of space, within which the gas pressure is lower than the pressure of the atmosphere surrounding it. A true vacuum — containing zero gas pressure — is considered impossible.

Gas contains moving molecules and gas pressure is the impact of these molecules on the wall of their environment. The other side of this wall is subject to the pressure of the gas (air) molecules that form the atmosphere.

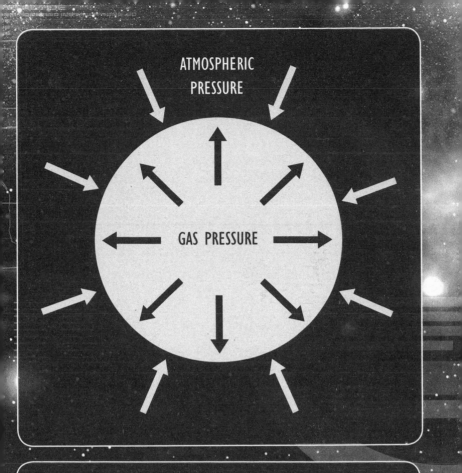

ATMOSPHERIC
PRESSURE

GAS PRESSURE

The higher atmospheric pressure pushes air into the vacuum. Other substances may be pushed by the air, for example, a pump is used to reduce the gas pressure inside a vacuum cleaner, and the air that is pushed in brings dirt with it. The same principle is used to draw milk from a cow's udders using a milking cup. When a person sucks at a drinking straw, gas pressure within the mouth is lowered, and air, pushed by the atmospheric pressure, forces the drink up the straw.

'But draining heads is a lot harder than nicking a nose. You can't put people to sleep before you do it, because the essential bit of them shuts down then. Somehow you've got to get people to look at you, stare deep into your eyes, and maintain that connection.'

Now he was addressing Mitra again. 'And Des gave you the perfect idea. A camera. People will stare into a camera for ages. You took one, modified it to become an extension of your own eyes – a sort of straw you could dip in the milkshake of their minds. Then you started sucking away. And you weren't taking in people who were bland and content. You were absorbing rock stars, actors, egotistical malcontents surging with ambition and drive. The more you took in, the more your personality built up, became whole, but the more you needed. Am I right?'

'Yes,' came a whisper. 'But you don't understand. The emptiness...'

The Doctor sighed. 'You're a real "soul half-empty" kind of girl, aren't you? Think of it as half full, appreciate all those stolen personalities already swirling around inside you.'

'No. I need more. I need you. There's so much inside

you. If I had that... I think I would be complete.'

'Just be content with what you've got! I mean, you could be a great photographer, taking normal pictures. I've seen your work! Although why you bothered delivering the photos when you'd already got a soul out of it...'

'Because it's what I took from the photographer's mind. And with that pretence, I might get access to more people.'

Mitra's voice was very close now. The Doctor thought he must be standing almost in front of her.

'I'm here!' Megan's whisper was close by too. 'I've got your coat.'

'Good girl,' the Doctor whispered back. 'Now, hand me the thing that's in the coat pocket, it's like a short metal rod.'

He reached out in front of him, and after a second felt the comforting presence of the sonic screwdriver in his grasp. He held it up –

And blaring out a hideous roaring screech, the screwdriver suddenly blazed bright blue, lighting up Mitra's camera, pointing straight at him.

The Doctor had a split second to realize that the alarm was warning him of a spaceship entering

Earth's atmosphere, before he found his gaze drawn to the lens.

'I've got you,' Mitra purred. 'Infrared filters in the camera, it's been working away at you all this time. Didn't you wonder why I was so quiet? I've been concentrating so hard. The process has been oh-so-slow in the darkness, but I've got enough of you already to stop you getting away. And now there is light I can finish the job quickly...' She twisted a dial on the top of the camera. 'Full power!'

# Villains Revealed

'Doctor!' cried Megan. 'Doctor, Doctor! Are you all right?'

'Yes,' said the Doctor dully. 'I am all right.'

The cold blue light showed Mitra's triumphant smile as she lowered the camera, swinging the strap on a single finger. 'And I'm brilliant!' she said.

The Doctor stared unblinkingly ahead. Then his mouth twitched. 'Brilliant?' he said with sudden animation. 'I'd say – fantastic!'

'What?' Mitra stumbled back in surprise. 'But I have you! I took every scrap of your personality from you!'

'Well, yeah, you did,' said the Doctor. 'Thing is – you didn't stop to check how many personalities I've got in there. That old vacuum trick works just as well inside me. One Doctor gone – another

109

one gets pushed out to fill the gap.' He reached forward and grabbed the camera from her. 'Now – say "cheese"!'

The Doctor was getting changed back into his own clothes in the wardrobe room. He and Megan had escaped from the frantic panic of the studio.

'There're a couple of people who were a lot nicer without their souls,' Megan commented. 'I don't think Pamela's ever gone that long without moaning at anyone before.'

'Sorry,' the Doctor said with a smile. 'All or nothing. As soon as I reversed the polarity of the camera, everything was just pushed out the other way. Mind you,' he added, adopting a confidential tone, 'between you and me, I wasn't a hundred per cent sure that all the personalities would find their way back to their right homes. Might have just flown into the nearest empty head.' He shuddered. 'I could have ended up with Pamela's mind inside me! Or any of them!'

'Or you could have ended up with two noses, or four ears!' Megan added.

The Doctor laughed. 'Compared to some of the faces I've had, that might have been an improvement...'

He clicked his tongue. 'No, everything's back with its rightful owner now.' He nodded towards the phone. 'Natasha says she's no longer nasally challenged, and the hospital says Mae Harrison's back to normal – and will recover from the accident. They haven't got a clue what to make of it, of course.'

'Lucky that with the camera on full power, it just sucked everything off of that Vacant woman,' said Megan.

The Doctor's smile fell away. 'Not lucky for her.' He looked down at the camera, lying on a table. He could see words written in white on the black plastic casing: the manufacturer's name and the camera model. The Ashkanazi MITRA. 'She didn't even have a name of her own. And anything she could call herself, any tiny scrap that wasn't stolen – it's in there, now. Trapped, unless I choose to let her – it – out.'

He did up the last button on his jacket, and picked up the camera by its strap. 'And I haven't decided yet if I'm going to do that.' He sighed. 'Anyway, I don't have time now to think about it. Nothing I'm about to say will make any sense to you, but... the first spaceship that entered the atmosphere will have arrived by now. And somehow I have to track down the giant empty space it's landed in before the second ship turns up, and I haven't got a clue where to go. Just that it's between here –' He pointed to his map – 'and here. Don't 'spose you know any great empty spaces around there?'

'Only the old studios,' Megan said. 'The ones where we used to film. It was a great big empty warehouse, but some weird things happened there and they said it was unsafe.'

'Unsafe? Weird things?' said the Doctor. 'The sort of things that might be caused by aliens scouting out a meeting location?'

'Er, could be, I suppose.'

The Doctor laughed out loud. 'Megan, you're brilliant!' He gave her a hug, and ran for the door.

She called after him: 'Doctor, there's no risk from other cameras now, is there?'

He stopped in the doorway and shook his head. She picked up a small digital camera and pointed it at him. 'Please? Just to remember you by? A memento of the soap star who never was?'

'Oh, go on then,' the Doctor agreed. She might just have saved the universe, he owed her something. He struck a pose.

Megan frowned. 'Hold on though, there's something missing...' She reached up to a hook, and pulled down the much-admired Admiral's hat. 'There you go, Cap'n!'

The Doctor saluted her as the camera clicked.

It was dark now, but the streets were still packed with people, some no doubt making their weary way home, others heading out for a night on the town. The Doctor weaved through the crowds, heading for the condemned Vienna Studios.

He thought back to his time on Karagula. It seemed so long ago! What had that Darksmith accused him of being? An agent of the K–? What were the K– when they were at home? Not the Karagulans – the Darksmiths themselves – they wouldn't need to make a deal with their own kind. What other races were there who might want such a terrible device? Koalas, Krynoids, Kandymen, Keytospons? None of them seemed likely.

The streets were less crowded now, the Doctor heading into a more out-of-the-way area of the city. Soon the buildings began to thin out too. Those that were left looked industrial and empty, huge cold boxes of grey concrete.

The Doctor drew in his breath. Three figures had just passed under one of the by-now-scarce streetlights. Two of the figures were tall and cloaked, one was shorter, slighter, female. Gisella.

All thoughts of Mitra the Vacant and the day's activities flew from the Doctor's mind. The adrenalin started to surge at the thought of his current mission. He had to get the Crystal – and, perhaps not as universally important, but crucial to the Doctor, he had to rescue Gisella, find a way of restoring her to her true self.

He followed the three figures as they ignored the 'Keep Out' signs and headed into a large concrete building. The Doctor ran on silent feet to the entrance, catching the door before it had fully shut behind them. He peered into the building.

The warehouse roof had been removed, and the enormous space within was now open to the stars. And from the stars had come a ship to fill it – a huge warship. He held his breath as a door opened in the ship and a ramp descended.

A nightmare creature appeared in the blank opening of the doorway, and began to descend the ramp. Another followed, and another.

The Doctor stared in horror at the figures that appeared from inside the alien spaceship that had landed amongst the ruined brickwork and rusted pipes of the warehouse.

'Krashoks!'

# To Be Continued...

To find out what events lie in store
for the Doctor and the mystery of the
Darksmith Legacy, look out for
The Art of War.
But for now, here is a taste of
things to come...

# DOCTOR · WHO

Book
9

# THE **DARKSMITH** LEGACY
## THE ART OF WAR

BY MIKE TUCKER

**www.thedarksmithlegacy.com**
Continue the amazing adventure online...

# Payment in Death

The Doctor shook his head. 'That's not good… Not good at all.'

Six of the Krashok warriors had now emerged from inside their ship. They looked like humans; at least they must have looked like humans once. Now they were an ugly mix of human being, robot and alien, mashed together like some strange jigsaw, each of them different from the next.

The Doctor had met them once – a long time ago, and a long way from Earth. He searched through his memory, trying to recall what he had learned about them.

They travelled the universe, searching for the most ferocious predators, the most successful fighters, taking the best bits from what they found and adding it to their own armoury. On the six

Krashoks standing before him, the Doctor could recognize parts from nearly eleven different alien species. One had the huge, clawed paws of a Renevian tiger, another the muscular arms and poison tip darts of a Slitheen, yet another the thin, spike-encrusted legs of a Gappa. Sharp teeth, barbed tails and razor sharp spines from across the universe had been stitched onto the Krashoks' bodies, held in place by ugly robotic clamps.

The only unifying feature that identified them all as Krashoks was the hard ruff of bony scales that fanned out from behind their necks, the rough plates dotted with trophies and insignia of rank. The more senior the Krashok the more highly decorated the ruff.

It wasn't simply their external appearance that had been changed. The Doctor knew from unpleasant experience that the inside of any Krashok was just as much of a jumble of alien species. Lungs that helped them breath poison gas, hearts protected with bony plates, stomachs that allowed them to eat practically anything without getting ill.

Each of the Krashok warriors had gleaming metal helmets bolted to their heads, laser sights and flickering screens covering their right eyes.

Backpacks bristling with weapons were slung across their shoulders, Dalek blasters, Cyberman guns, Rinteppi bazookas. The Krashok collected weapons from all over the galaxy. Anything to ensure that they were the superior fighting force in the universe, and that they had product to sell.

'Yes,' the Doctor murmured to himself. 'It makes sense. The Krashoks develop weapons, and then they start wars and sell the weapons that they've built to both sides. They are the ones who commissioned the Darksmiths in the first place!'

He shook his head angrily. The Krashoks were about to engineer another war. With the Eternity Crystal finally recovered and Varlos's machine complete the Krashoks would enable each side to keep raising their dead from the battlefield and the war would rage for centuries. An unending marketplace for the Krashoks and never mind who got caught in the crossfire and fallout.

The Doctor's jaw tightened. He had been through one war that had torn the universe apart. He wasn't about to sit by and let another one start.

He ducked down into the shadows of the warehouse as two more Krashoks emerged from the ship. These two were even more heavily armoured than their fellow warriors, their patchwork skins rough from the scars of battle, their neck ruffs encrusted with the insignia of rank. War Commanders. All Krashok campaigns were organized by two Commanders, each dealing with one of the opposing sides, both orchestrating the maximum carnage from behind the scenes.

As they appeared, the Darksmiths waiting for them bowed low. The Krashok leaders gave each other a sly grin, one revealing huge, yellowing tusks, the other gleaming metal fangs as their lips curled back.

'High Minister Drakon. A pleasure to see you again,' said one.

'I trust you have the Crystal?' hissed the other.

The High Minister pulled back the cowl of his cape, revealing his pale, skull-like face. With his skin pulled tight across his teeth it was impossible to tell if he was smiling or not.

'Commander Grelt. Commander Skraar,' he nodded at each in turn. 'But of course we have brought the Crystal. Would we have agreed to meet you on this... disagreeable planet if we had not?'

'Who knows what is in the mind of a Darksmith?' sneered Grelt. 'You have, after all, already left us waiting for millennia.'

'And that has lost us a lot of money, Drakon,' Skraar clumped down the ramp, towering over the frail body of the Darksmith. 'So where is the Crystal?'

Drakon waved a skeletal hand at Gisella. As the Doctor watched she stepped forward, holding out the case in her hands, snapping open the clasps and pulling open the lid.

The Krashok commanders hissed in pleasure, their patchwork faces lit up by the pale glow of the Eternity Crystal. Skraar reached out with a huge claw, but Drakon snapped the box shut sharply. Gisella looked at him, her pale face creasing with puzzlement. Skraar gave a snarl of displeasure, his hand reaching for the massive blaster that hung from his belt.

'Please, Commander,' Drakon held his hands up disarmingly. 'There's no need for any unpleasantness. The Crystal is here as agreed, but before you take possession of it there is the matter of payment to be discussed.'

Commander Grelt placed a huge armoured hand on the shoulder of his fellow Commander.

'Drakon has made a reasonable enough request.

We should pay him what he is due.'

Skraar's hand relaxed from the butt of the blaster.

'Indeed.' He smiled. 'We have both waited long enough for this moment, a few more minutes will make no difference.'

From his hiding place the Doctor's mind was racing. In a matter of moments the Krashoks would have the Eternity Crystal inside their ship and this would all be over. He had to stop them!

He stared around at the crumbling ruins of the warehouse. High above him, rusting metal beams crisscrossed the grey of the night sky, all that remained of the collapsed roof. The Doctor's gaze flicked back and forth between the open roof and the gleaming bulk of the Krashok ship.

His eyes narrowed. The huge battlecruiser could have only just fit through the gap. If he could narrow that gap…

Pulling his sonic screwdriver from his jacket pocket he slipped his glasses onto his nose and squinted upwards, searching for weak points in the ruined roof.

# DOCTOR · WHO

## THE DARKSMITH LEGACY

## 'Collected' Party

Celebrate the epic Darksmith Legacy experience with an out-of-this-world party to be held in a secret London location during the October half-term 2009, after the final exciting instalment has been published.

For your chance to win an exclusive ticket to this Doctor Who Extravaganza you must sign up at www.thedarksmithlegacy.com, complete the quest online and submit your details. We will let you know if you have been successful via email.

This will be a once in a lifetime opportunity to win lots of Doctor Who prizes and see scary monsters up-close...

...Don't miss out!

More party details will be revealed in another dimension on the Darksmith website so keep checking back for further updates. Full Terms and Conditions can also be found at www.thedarksmithlegacy.com.

# DOCTOR · WHO

## Fantastic free Doctor Who slipcase offer when you buy two Darksmith Legacy books!

### Limited to the first 500 respondents!

To be eligible to receive your free slipcase, fill in your details on the form below and send along with original receipt(s) showing the purchase of two Darksmith Legacy books. The first 500 correctly completed forms will receive a slipcase.

Offer subject to availability. Terms and conditions apply. See overleaf for details.

Here – – – – – – – – – – – – – – – – – – – – – –

## Entry Form

Name: ...............................................................................................................

Address: ...........................................................................................................

Email: ..............................................................................................................

Have you remembered to include your two original sales receipts? ⬡

I have read and agree to the terms and conditions overleaf. ⬡

Tick here if you don't want to receive marketing communications from Penguin Brands and Licensing. ⬡

### Important – Are you over 13 years old?

If you are 13 or over just tick this box, you don't need to do anything else. ⬡

If you are under 13, you must get your parent or guardian to enter the promotion on your behalf. If they agree, please show them the notice below.

### Notice to parent/guardian of entrants under 13 years old

If you are a parent/guardian of the entrant and you consent to the retention and use of the entrant's personal details by Penguin Brands and Licensing for the purposes of this promotion, please tick this box. ⬡

Name of parent/guardian: .................................................................................

**Terms and Conditions**

1. This promotion is subject to availability and is limited to the first 500 correctly completed respondents received.
2. This promotion is open to all residents aged 7 years or over in the UK, with the exception of employees of the Promoter, their immediate families and anyone else connected with this promotion. Entries from entrants under the age of 13 years must be made by a parent/guardian on their behalf.
3. The Promoter accepts no responsibility for any entries that are incomplete, illegal or fail to reach the promoter for any reason. Proof of sending is not proof of receipt. Entries via agents or third parties are invalid.
4. Only one entry per person. No entrant may receive more than one slipcase.
5. To enter, fill in your details on the entry form and send along with original sales receipt(s) showing purchase of two Doctor Who: The Darksmith Legacy books to: Doctor Who Slipcase Offer, Brands and Licensing, 80 Strand, London, WC2R 0RL.
6. The first 500 correctly completed entries will receive a slipcase.
7. Offer only available on purchases of Doctor Who: The Darksmith Legacy books.
8. Please allow 31days for receipt of your slip case.
9. Slip cases are subject to availability. In the event of exceptional circumstances, the Promoter reserves the right to amend or foreclose the promotion without notice. No correspondence will be entered into.
10. All instructions given on the entry form, form part of the terms and conditions.
11. The Promoter will use any data submitted by entrants for only the purposes of running the promotion, unless otherwise stated in the entry details. By entering this promotion, all entrants consent to the use of their personal data by the Promoter for the purposes of the administration of this promotion and any other purposes to which the entrant has consented.
12. By entering this promotion, each entrant agrees to be bound by these terms and conditions.
13. The Promoter is Penguin Books Limited, 80 Strand, London WC2R 0RL.

Cut Here

# Doctor Who Slipcase Offer
Brands and Licensing
80 Strand
London
WC2R 0RL